All rights reserved. Published by Scholastic Inc., *Publishers since 1920.*
SCHOLASTIC and associated logos are trademarks and/or registered
trademarks of Scholastic Inc.

The publisher does not have any control over and does not assume any
responsibility for author or third-party websites or their content.

This book is a work of fiction. Names, characters, places, and
incidents are either the product of the author's imagination or
are used fictitiously, and any resemblance to actual persons,
living or dead, business establishments, events, or locales
is entirely coincidental.

ISBN 978-1-338-23650-7

10 9 8 7 6 5 4 3 2 1   17 18 19 20 21

Printed and bound in Italy

First edition, December 2017

Written by Emily Stead

Scholastic Inc., 557 Broadway, New York, NY 10012

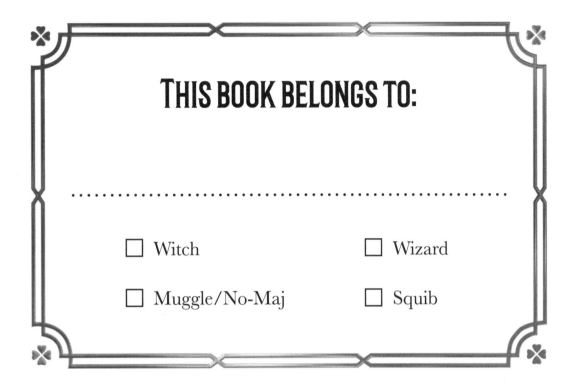

THIS BOOK BELONGS TO:

. . . .

☐ Witch   ☐ Wizard

☐ Muggle/No-Maj ☐ Squib

J.K. ROWLING'S
Wizarding World

A MAGICAL YEARBOOK

A CINEMATIC JOURNEY: IMAGINE, DRAW, CREATE

CONTENTS

Welcome to the Wizarding World...   9

Fantastic Beasts and Where to Find Them   11
Newt Scamander   12
New York City   14
Fantastic Beasts Postcards   15

**The Wizarding World Guide
to Wands and Spells**   16

MACUSA   17
The New Salem Philanthropic Society   18
New York Friends   20
Fit for a Queen   21
Meet the Beasts   22
Naughty Niffler   24
Newt Scamander Poster   25
Fantastic Beasts Poster   26
Danger in the City   27
The Obscurus   28

Harry Potter   31
Beginnings   32
Owl Post   33
Friends and Foes   34
Houses of Hogwarts   36
Houses of Hogwarts Postcards   37
Famous Faces   39
Powerful Potions   40
Caring for Creatures   41
Triwizard Tournament   42
Young Love   44
Who Suits Who?   45
Quidditch   46
Hidden Horcruxes   48
The Life of Albus Dumbledore   50
Lord Voldemort: a Timeline   52
Dementors   54
Order of the Phoenix   56
Dumbledore's Army   57
The Deathly Hallows   58
Death Eaters   59
The Battle of Hogwarts   60

WELCOME TO THE
WIZARDING WORLD...

… a magical community of witches and wizards. Life in the wizarding world is kept hidden from the non-magical community, a world inhabited by Muggles and No-Majs.

The wizarding world is bound by the International Statute of Wizarding Secrecy, which forbids witches and wizards to reveal anything about magic or perform charms or spells while in non-wizarding society. If something of a magical nature is accidentally revealed, there's always the Obliviate Charm to erase a Muggle's memories.

Most witches and wizards have a form of wizarding government to oversee magical affairs in their territory, such as the Ministry of Magic in the UK or the Magical Congress of the United States of America (MACUSA).

The proper education of witches and wizards is crucial, too. Some of the most prestigious wizarding schools in the world include Hogwarts School of Witchcraft and Wizardry, Ilvermorny School of Witchcraft and Wizardry, Beauxbatons Academy of Magic and Durmstrang Institute.

Read on to imagine your own magical journey through the wizarding world…

FANTASTIC
BEASTS
AND WHERE
TO FIND THEM™

'NEWT'
NEWTON ARTEMIS FIDO SCAMANDER

Newt Scamander comes from a well-established, English wizarding family and studied at Hogwarts School of Witchcraft and Wizardry. He is a Magizoologist.

Newt travels the world to find and document magical creatures for his book *Fantastic Beasts and Where to Find Them*. He wants to educate the wizarding community about why these creatures are important and need to be protected.

Newt arrives in New York City in 1926, with nothing more than the clothes on his back and a modest leather case. But his is no ordinary case – it is also the home to a fantastic array of magical creatures!

Imagine you were going on a trip to search for fantastic beasts. What would you take with you? Sketch the items in the case below.

In the Great War, Newt worked in the Beast Division for the Ministry of Magic programme where he handled and trained Ukrainian Ironbelly dragons.

NEW YORK CITY

New York was the cultural, financial and industrial capital of the United States during the 1920s. Jazz music, nightclubs and a fast-paced lifestyle made the 1920s 'roar' after the bleak years of the Great War.

Newt's travels take him to New York City. What was supposed to be a brief stopover turns into a lengthier stay when Newt's case is unintentionally switched and his magical creatures are accidentally released in the city!

Newt's visit comes at a time when relations between magical and non-magical communities are at an all-time low, as the New Salem Philanthropic Society calls for a purge of wizardkind.

IT'S CHARMING!

NEW YORK

MAGICAL
CONGRESS
OF THE USA

A MAGICAL
WELCOME

TO
NEW YORK

Fly to New York for...
...a Broom with a View

MACUSA

The Magical Congress of the United States of America, or MACUSA, is the body in the United States that polices and protects American witches and wizards. Created in 1693, it is the equivalent of the UK's Ministry of Magic.

MAGICAL EXPOSURE THREAT LEVEL

EMERGENCY
LEVEL 6

SEVERE: UNEXPLAINED ACTIVITY

DANGER
LEVEL 4

HIGH ALERT
LEVEL 3

MODERATE
LEVEL 2

LOW THREAT
LEVEL 1

ZERO THREAT

WITCH HUNTS	537
EXPOSURES	082
OBLIVIATIONS	910

When Newt arrives in New York, a Dark presence is terrorizing the city. He must prove to MACUSA that his escaped magical creatures are not to blame, and that a Dark and sinister force is at play.

The magical exposure threat level clock denotes a 'severe' situation, due to the unexplained attacks in the city.

THE NEW SALEM PHILANTHROPIC SOCIETY

The New Salem Philanthropic Society's (NSPS) main aim is to inform the public about 'dangerous' witches and wizards that live among them. Known as Second Salemers, these extreme No-Majs are desperate to bring back the Salem witch trials from centuries ago.

The NSPS's leader is Mary Lou Barebone.

Chastity, Modesty and Credence are Mary Lou's adopted children. They are tasked with recruiting more followers to the join the society's cause.

WITCHES LIVE AMONG US!

Mary Lou Barebone uses posters and pamphlets to recruit members to her army of Second Salemers. Imagine if you were recruiting people to join a society of your own. What would it be called? Design a poster that would help recruit people to your society.

NEW YORK FRIENDS

During his visit, Newt encounters some unusual New Yorkers – one is even a Muggle, or No-Maj, as he's known in America. Little does Newt know that these unlikely acquaintances will become great friends.

Newt meets aspiring baker and No-Maj Jacob Kowalski at a local bank. After their cases accidentally get switched, Jacob proves to be enormously helpful in tracking down Newt's runaway beasts.

BOTH SISTERS ATTENDED ILVERMORNY SCHOOL OF WITCHCRAFT AND WIZARDRY.

No-Majs! No-Magics non-Wizards

As an Auror, Porpentina 'Tina' Goldstein excelled at investigating crimes committed against the wizarding community. However, her attack on a No-Maj due to her unwillingness to move past one particular, controversial case, led to her eventual demotion to the Wand Permit Office at MACUSA.

Glamorous Queenie Goldstein works alongside her older sister Tina at MACUSA. Queenie is a Legilimens, which means she possesses the rare ability to read other people's thoughts.

FIT FOR A QUEEN

Queenie always dresses to impress! Design a stylish outfit below that you could imagine Queenie wearing.

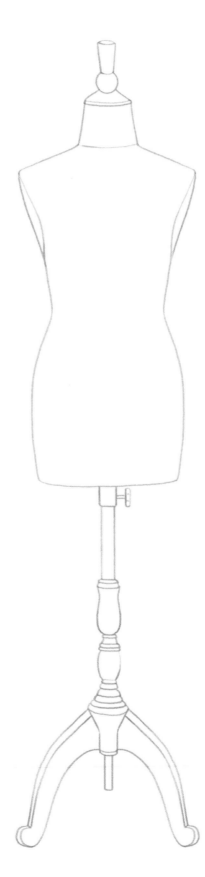

MEET THE BEASTS

From the pocket-sized Bowtruckle to the thunderous Erumpent that can blast through brick walls, Newt has set up peaceful habitats in his case for each rescued beast to live freely. He cares for them as deeply as if he were their own mother.

NIFFLER

This long-snouted rodent-like creature is attracted to anything shiny. Its treasures are collected in an unfeasibly large pouch in its belly.

DEMIGUISE

These creatures have the ability to become invisible at will and have precognitive sight making them extremely hard to recapture.

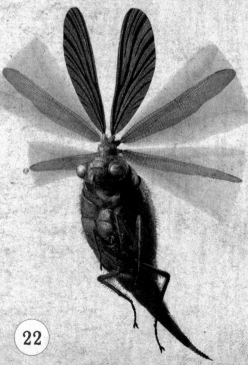

BILLYWIG

Billywigs are small blue creatures with helicopter-like wings on their heads.

NEWT HAS BUILT HABITATS CALLED BIOMES FOR EACH BEAST AND KEEPS CAREFUL RECORDS OF EACH CREATURE'S FEEDING NEEDS USING A SPECIAL CHART.

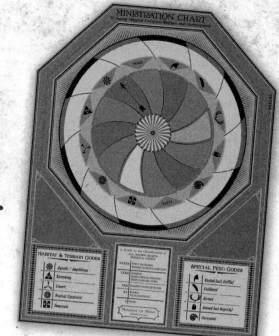

ERUMPENT

This huge, powerful beast has a hide so thick, it can repel most spells and charms. Treat an Erumpent with caution!

MURTLAP

Murtlaps are rat-like creatures with an anemone-like growth on their backs.

BOWTRUCKLE

Newt is particularly fond of Pickett, a cute and needy Bowtruckle that he keeps safe in his breast pocket.

NAUGHTY NIFFLER

The Niffler is perhaps the escapee that causes the most trouble for Newt during his short visit. It can't help but steal anything that sparkles! Finish colouring this mischievous creature and don't forget to add the sparkly items in its paws.

DANGER CITY IN THE

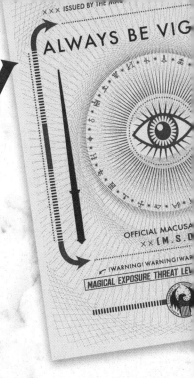

During Newt's visit to New York, danger seems to lurk around every corner. Decide which you think pose the greatest threat to our Magizoologist by numbering the sentences below from 1–5, with 1 being the least dangerous and 5 being the most.

- ☐ ESCAPED CREATURES, SUCH AS THE RAMPANT ERUMPENT.

- ☐ MACUSA OFFICIALS WHO TRY TO IMPRISON HIM.

- ☐ THE RETURN OF THE DARK WIZARD, GELLERT GRINDELWALD.

- ☐ THE RADICAL MARY LOU BAREBONE, WHO FIRMLY CRUSADES AGAINST THE WIZARDS AND WITCHES.

- ☐ THE OBSCURUS, A DARK AND VIOLENT FORCE THAT MANIFESTS ITSELF WHEN A CHILD BORN WITH MAGICAL POWERS SUPPRESSES HIS OR HER ABILITIES.

THE Obscurus

This dark, snarling shadow attacks as swiftly as it vanishes. Its energy is powerful enough to cause major destruction to anything in its path, including buildings, cars and innocent bystanders.

 THIS EMERGENCY MESSAGE SHOWS HOW THE CITY IS IN GREAT DANGER.

The Shaw family's fundraiser is cut short when the Obscurus rushes into the room.

MACUSA CODE NO: 1   5   10   20

→ **EMERGENCY MESSAG**
××× ISSUED BY THE MACUSA SURVEILLANCE DEPARTM

↵ !WARNING! WARNING! WARNING! WARNIN

MAGICAL EXPOSURE THREAT LEVEL HAS REACH

UNEXPLAINED ACTIVITY
→ DO NOT LET IT REACH: LEVEL 6

(5) PRESIDENT SERAPHINA PICQUERY WILL ADDRESS THE WIZARDING COMMUNITY BY
LETTER. IF YOU REQUIRE MORE INFORMATION PLEASE CONTACT THE MACUSA
SURVEILLANCE WIZARDING RESOURCES DEPARTMENT (M.S.W.R.D).
THEY WILL BE ABLE TO PROVIDE SUPPORT AND ADVISE YOU ON HOW TO STAY SAFE.
EMERGENCY. FURTHER ADVICE CAN ALSO BE FOUND IN MACUSA / SAFETY
IN THE WORKPLACE.

◆ ALWAYS BE VIGILANT ◆

28

TRANSFIGURATION TODAY

EDITION 2085

2/6

THE MAGAZINE THAT CHANGES LIVES

REVEALED!

?

40 60 80 20 100

EXPOSED!

Imagine that you are the writer of this top wizarding magazine and you've been tasked with writing about the Obscurus. Draw pictures and write a headline that tells the story.

BEGINNINGS

Although lots of unexplained things happened to Harry earlier in his life, Harry only discovered he was a wizard on his eleventh birthday. This news would change his life forever.

Harry is delivered to the Dursleys as a baby after Lord Voldemort killed his parents, Lily and James Potter.

Hundreds of letters addressed to Harry Potter fly down the chimney of number four Privet Drive.

Eventually, a letter from Hogwarts School of Witchcraft and Wizardry will always reach the wizard or witch for whom it was intended.

Owl Post

Imagine you could send Harry a letter by Owl Post before his first term starts. What sort of questions would you want to ask him?

FRIENDS AND FOES

First impressions, although not always right, can be just as important in the wizarding world as in Muggle society. Harry must decide who he can trust during his first term at Hogwarts.

The first member of the magical community that Harry meets is half-giant, Rubeus Hagrid.

Fellow Gryffindor Ron forms a strong friendship with Harry.

Muggle-born Hermione has a talent for magic and spellwork.

Albus Dumbledore is Hogwarts' long-standing Headmaster.

Slytherin Draco Malfoy comes from a wealthy wizarding family.

Head of Slytherin house, Professor Snape, appears to take an instant dislike to Harry.

Gryffindor's Head, Professor Minerva McGonagall, is stern but fair.

HOGWARTS

DRACO DORMIENS NUNQUAM TITILLANDUS

HOUSES OF
HOGWARTS

The ancient Sorting Hat places students into one of four famous houses upon entry into Hogwarts. Which house do you think the Sorting Hat would choose for you? Read the descriptions below then circle which one suits you best.

GRYFFINDOR

The virtues of courage, bravery and determination are valued highly by Gryffindors.

HUFFLEPUFF

Hufflepuffs are not afraid to work hard. They are known for their loyalty, kindness and tolerance.

RAVENCLAW

Learning, wit and wisdom are important ideals to Ravenclaws.

SLYTHERIN

The house of Slytherin produces leaders who are resourceful, ambitious and cunning.

GRYFFINDOR™

HUFFLEPUFF™

RAVENCLAW™

SLYTHERIN™

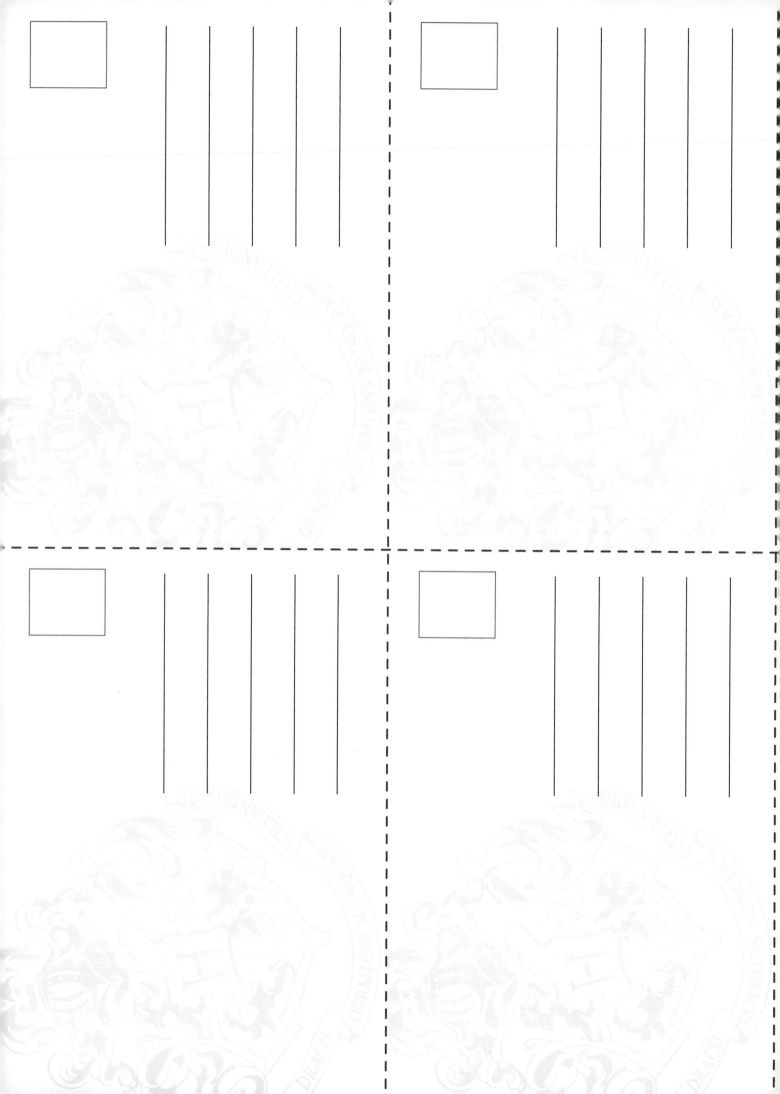

FAMOUS FACES

🦡 Hufflepuff

Cedric Diggory, Pomona Sprout and Newt Scamander were placed in Hufflepuff house.

🦁 Gryffindor

Godric Gryffindor, Harry Potter and the Weasley family are among some of the well-known Gryffindors.

🦅 Ravenclaw

Luna Lovegood, Cho Chang and Gilderoy Lockhart are all talented Ravenclaws.

🐍 Slytherin

Famous Slytherins include founder Salazar Slytherin, the Malfoy family, Bellatrix Lestrange and Tom Riddle.

POWERFUL POTIONS

From Polyjuice Potion to Felix Felicis, the cauldrons are always brewing in Potions class at Hogwarts. If you could brew a powerful potion from the list below, which one would you choose?

Polyjuice Potion (transforms the drinker into another person) ——————— ☐

Ageing Potion (ages the drinker, according to how much is consumed) ——— ☐

Amortentia (makes the drinker fall in love with the first person they see) —— ☐

Veritaserum (makes the drinker tell the truth) ——————————— ☐

Now imagine you could make a potion of your very own. What would you call it and what would it do? Name: _____ Effect: _____

Draw your potion below:

Professor Snape is Potions Master in Harry's first few years at Hogwarts.

CARING FOR Creatures

Third-year students at Hogwarts can elect to take Care of Magical Creatures class. The main textbook used is *Fantastic Beasts and Where to Find Them*, written by former Hogwarts student, Newt Scamander.

Professor: Rubeus Hagrid

Harry in his lesson on Hippogriffs.

Harry encounters Thestrals with Luna Lovegood in the Forbidden Forest.

A centaur is an intelligent magical creature that is half-human, half-horse.

TRIWIZARD TOURNAMENT

When Hogwarts hosts this magical contest in Harry's fourth year, the tournament proves more of a test than anyone could have imagined. Three wizarding schools compete to win the Triwizard Cup.

Durmstrang

School: Durmstrang Institute

Location: believed to be situated in the far north of Europe

Champion: Viktor Krum

Hogwarts

School: Hogwarts School of Witchcraft and Wizardry

Location: United Kingdom

Champions: Cedric Diggory and Harry Potter

Beauxbatons

School: Beauxbatons Academy of Magic

Location: thought to be in the Pyrenees

Champion: Fleur Delacour

Young LOVE

The course of true love never runs smoothly … especially at Hogwarts!

During her fourth year, Hermione attends the Yule Ball with Viktor Krum.

Harry and Cho Chang grow close as members of Dumbledore's Army.

Lavender Brown is sweet on Ron in their sixth year at Hogwarts, though the relationship soon fizzles out.

In Harry Potter and the Deathly Hallows – Part 1, Ginny Weasley is revealed to be Harry's true love.

It takes Ron and Hermione a long time to realize they would make the perfect partnership.

WHO Suits WHO?

Draw a line to the partner you think best suits each of our heroes.

Cho

Harry

Ginny

Lavender

Ron

Hermione

Hermione

Viktor

Ron

QUIDDITCH

The magical game Quidditch has been played for centuries in the wizarding world. Fast-paced and brutal, it is Harry's favourite sport.

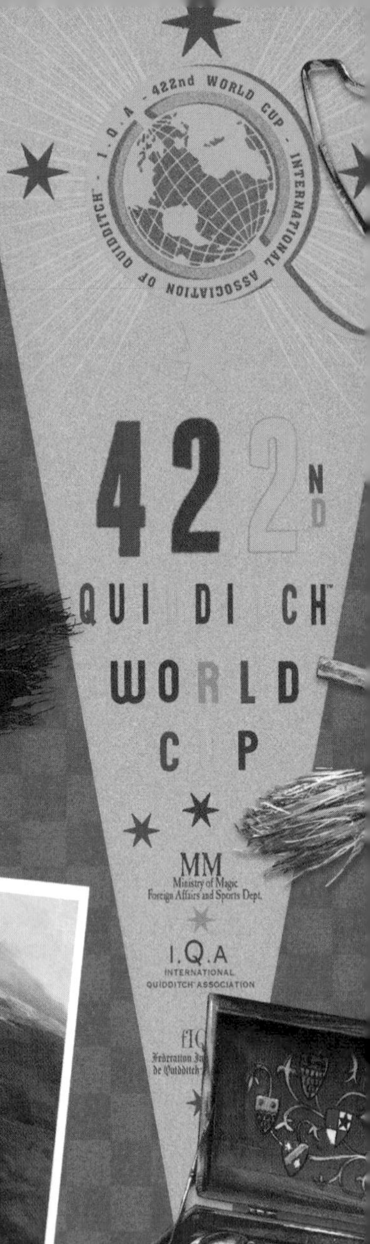

42 2ND
QUI DI CH
WORLD
C P

MM
Ministry of Magic
Foreign Affairs and Sports Dept.

I.Q.A
INTERNATIONAL
QUIDDITCH ASSOCIATION

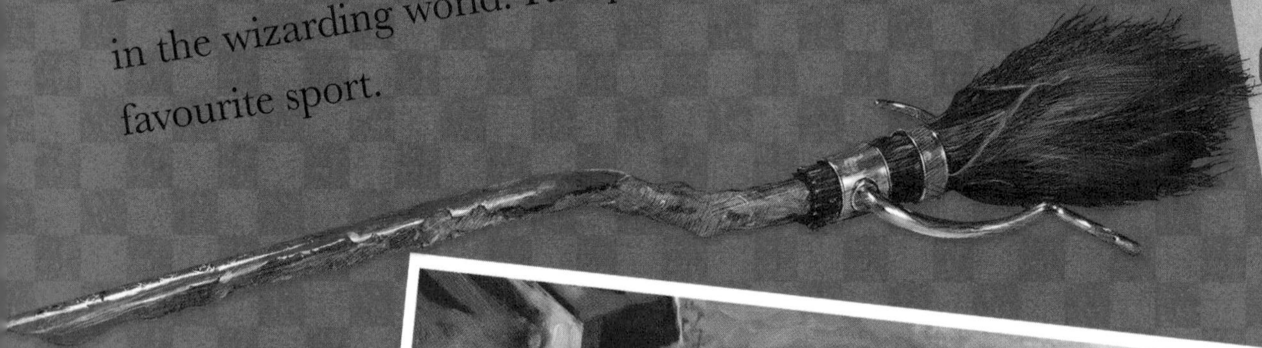

fIQ
Federation Internationale
de Quidditch

Nimbus
RACING BROOMS

Harry, Ron and Ginny all play on the Gryffindor Quidditch team. Design a new kit you could imagine your dream Quidditch team wearing. Don't forget to draw a broom!

Which Hogwarts Quidditch team would you most like to play against?

Gryffindor ☐

Ravenclaw ☐

Hufflepuff ☐

Slytherin ☐

HIDDEN Horcruxes

A Horcrux is an object or living thing into which a wizard or witch puts part of his or her soul so they can live on even if their body is destroyed. They can only be created after a murder has been committed. Lord Voldemort made seven Horcruxes and Harry had to find them all before he could defeat the Dark Lord.

1. TOM RIDDLE'S DIARY
- Slipped into Ginny Weasley's cauldron by Lucius Malfoy at Flourish and Blotts
- Destroyed by Harry Potter with the Basilisk fang in the Chamber of Secrets

2. MARVOLO GAUNT'S RING
- Voldemort's family ring
- Destroyed by Albus Dumbledore

3. SALAZAR SLYTHERIN'S LOCKET
- Tracked down by Harry, Ron and Hermione at the Ministry of Magic
- Destroyed by Ron Weasley with the Sword of Gryffindor

4. Helga Hufflepuff's Cup

- Discovered in Bellatrix Lestrange's vault at Gringotts
- Destroyed by Hermione Granger with the Basilisk fang in the Chamber of Secrets

5. Rowena Ravenclaw's Diadem

- Hidden in Hogwarts' Room of Requirement
- Stabbed by Harry Potter with the Basilisk fang and kicked by Ron Weasley into the Fiendfyre

6. Nagini

- Voldemort's huge pet snake and loyal servant
- Killed by Neville Longbottom with the Sword of Gryffindor

7. Harry Potter

- The rebound of Voldemort's Killing Curse accidently created a Horcrux in Harry himself
- Destroyed by Voldemort when he casts the Killing Curse on Harry again

THE LIFE OF
Albus Dumbledore

Hogwarts' Headmaster Albus Dumbledore was one of the most powerful wizards ever to have lived. How much do you know about the great professor?

Full name: Albus Percival Wulfric Brian Dumbledore

Born: 1881

Parents: Percival and Kendra Dumbledore, a witch and a wizard

Siblings: a younger brother, Aberforth and sister, Ariana

When Albus is eleven, he begins studying at Hogwarts and is sorted into Gryffindor.

After his mother dies, he returns to Godric's Hollow to care for his brother and sister. He soon becomes friends with Gellert Grindelwald, another young wizard visiting the area.

Ariana was accidentally killed in a duel between Aberforth and Gellert. Albus blames himself for her death.

Albus becomes a professor at Hogwarts and later meets Tom Riddle, a troubled young man. He brings him to Hogwarts.

Gellert Grindelwald gains power as a Dark wizard. Dumbledore knows he has to defeat Grindelwald and take possession of the stolen Elder Wand.

Tom Riddle rises to power as Lord Voldemort. Dumbledore forms the Order of the Phoenix, a secret society to fight him.

When Voldemort attacks and kills Lily and James Potter, Dumbledore feels a duty to protect their son, Harry, who survived Voldemort's attack.

Harry is sent to live with his Muggle relatives, the Dursleys, but when he turns eleven, he is given a place at Hogwarts. Dumbledore watches over Harry there, giving him an Invisibility Cloak that belonged to Harry's father.

When Voldemort uses Harry's blood to regenerate his body and regain his powers, Dumbledore calls together the old Order of the Phoenix to fight the Dark Lord.

Dumbledore is removed as Hogwarts' Headmaster when he takes responsibility for forming Dumbledore's Army.

Dumbledore battles Voldemort in the Ministry of Magic's HQ, but does not kill him. He is reinstated as Headmaster when the Minister for Magic, Cornelius Fudge, is forced to admit he was wrong about Voldemort.

Dumbledore endures many challenges to obtain Voldemort's Horcruxes, leaving him in a weakened state.

A frail Dumbledore and Harry return from the cave where one of Voldemort's Horcruxes was kept to find the Dark Mark over the school. Dumbledore is disarmed by Draco Malfoy, but killed by Severus Snape at the top of the Astronomy Tower. He is buried at Hogwarts, near the Great Lake.

Lord VOLDEMORT: A TIMELINE

How well do you know the Dark Lord? Read this terrifying timeline of the events in his life.

Full name: Tom Marvolo Riddle
Born: 31st December 1926
Parents: Tom Riddle Senior and Merope Gaunt, a Muggle and a witch
Siblings: none

After his father abandons his mother and she dies shortly after his birth, Tom Riddle is raised in an orphanage.

Aged eleven, he goes to study at Hogwarts, and is sorted into Slytherin. He soon becomes a brilliant wizard and a school prefect. Tom turns to Dark magic and reinvents himself as Lord Voldemort upon leaving Hogwarts.

When a baby is born to Lily and James Potter, Voldemort believes the child has the power to destroy him. He murders the Potters, but his attempt to kill Harry backfires. Voldemort is ripped from his body and forced into hiding.

During Harry's first year at Hogwarts, Voldemort's spirit, attached to Professor Quirrell, fails to steal the Philosopher's Stone.

The following year, Ginny Weasley finds the diary of Tom Riddle. The memory of Tom possesses her and makes her open the Chamber of Secrets. Harry defeats Voldemort in the chamber, when he destroys both the Basilisk and the diary.

Harry and Voldemort come face to face in their first duel during the third task of the Triwizard Tournament. Voldemort is unable to defeat Harry.

In Harry's fifth year, Voldemort lures Harry into the Hall of Prophecy in the Department of Mysteries, and duels with Dumbledore.

Lord Voldemort dies in the Battle of Hogwarts, when hit by his own curse in the Great Hall.

DEMENTORS

Dementors are Dark creatures that guard Azkaban prison. Dementors feed on a person's positive emotions, draining these feelings from their victims. They suck out a person's soul with their deathly Dementor's Kiss.

Chilling Dementors wreak havoc on the Hogwarts Express.

Chocolate is sometimes given to revive a victim of a Dementor encounter.

Harry gets close to suffering a hideous Dementor's kiss.

Luna Lovegood summoning her Patronus.

The Patronus Charm conjures an animal guardian to defend against a Dementor attack. To cast this powerful defensive spell, the witch or wizard must recall a memory of when they were most happy or hopeful.

Think of your own happiest memories then write them below.

If you could conjure a Patronus, which animal form do you think it might take?

cat ☐   stag ☐   dragon ☐   dog ☐

bat ☐   owl ☐   other:

Harry conjures his stag Patronus when faced with hundreds of Dementors at the Great Lake.

⊕RDER
OF THE PHOENIX

The Order of the Phoenix is a secret society, led by Dumbledore. It is made up of wizards that oppose Lord Voldemort. How many of the members below do you think you can you name? Draw a line from each name in the list to one of the portraits below.

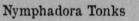
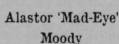
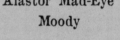

Molly Weasley

Nymphadora Tonks   Arthur Weasley

Rubeus Hagrid

Alastor 'Mad-Eye'   Kingsley
Moody   Shacklebolt

Minerva
McGonagall

Remus Lupin   Albus
                                     Dumbledore

Sirius Black

Now imagine if you could be part of the

ORDER OF THE PHOENIX

Draw a picture of yourself in the blank frame.

DUMBLEDORE'S ARMY

After Lord Voldemort returns at the end of Harry's fourth year, Harry secretly teaches his friends how to protect themselves using Defence Against the Dark Arts magic.

Neville Longbottom rallies the troops once more in their final year, when Hogwarts falls under Voldemort's control.

The DA, as it is known, must meet in secret, as Professor Umbridge's Inquisitorial Squad loiter around every corner.

THE DEATHLY HALLOWS

The Deathly Hallows are three powerful magical objects said to make the owner the Master of Death. They include the Elder Wand, which gives a witch or wizard more power than any other, the Resurrection Stone, which has the power to bring back the dead and the Invisibility Cloak, which when worn can make the user invisible.

Imagine you came into possession of one of the Deathly Hallows. Which item would you want the most? What would you do with it?

Invisibility Cloak   Resurrection Stone   Elder Wand

DeathEATERS

Death Eaters, the followers of Lord Voldemort, are made up of witches and wizards who practise the Dark Arts. Circle the witch or wizard below whose loyalty may not lie with the Dark Lord.

Voldemort's followers

Bellatrix Lestrange

Lucius Malfoy

Severus Snape

The Dark Mark is a symbol of loyalty to the Dark Lord that Death Eaters have branded on their left forearm. It is also used as a form of magical communication between Voldemort and his followers.

THE BATTLE OF HOGWARTS

The Battle of Hogwarts was one of the darkest days in wizarding history, as Voldemort and his Death Eaters stormed the school.

The Order of the Phoenix stands strong.

Voldemort weakens once the final Horcrux is destroyed.

Harry is able to destroy the Dark Lord, once and for all.